DOLORES MEETS HER MATCH

Barbara Samuels

Melanie Kroupa Books

Farrar, Straus and Giroux / New York

For Melanie with love
from Dolores

Distributed in Canada by Douglas & McIntyre Ltd.
Color separations by Chroma Graphics PTE Ltd.
Printed and bound in China by South China Printing Co. Ltd.
Designed by Jay Colvin
First edition, 2007
1 3 5 7 9 10 8 6 4 2

www.fsgkidsbooks.com

Library of Congress Cataloging-in-Publication Data
Samuels, Barbara.
    Dolores meets her match / Barbara Samuels.— 1st ed.
        p.   cm.
    Summary: Although new girl Hillary's pedigreed Siamese kitten can meow
seven different ways, Dolores loves her own cat, Duncan, who is very talented
at napping.
    ISBN-13: 978-0-374-31758-4
    ISBN-10: 0-374-31758-5
    [1. Cats—Fiction.   2. Pets—Fiction.]   I. Title.

PZ7.S1925 Dk 2007
[E]—dc22

                                                                            2006048950

Everybody who knew Dolores
had heard about . . .

her amazing cat, Duncan.

They learned how brave . . .

Duncan saves me from a waterbug!

and kind . . .

Duncan keeps my toes warm when it's chilly.

and helpful he could be.

Duncan does his part on fish night.

The end

One day, a new girl joined the class.

"Hi!" she said. "My name is Hillary."

Soon they learned all about Harold, her Siamese kitten. Harold had a long line of distinguished relatives. Hillary brought in a copy of his pedigree and some family photos to prove it.

SHOW-AND-TELL

HAROLD

Grandma Edwina, famous beauty

Father, Sir Percival Pym

Uncle Ferdie, Grand Champion

Best In Show

Cousin Maude, fashion trendsetter

"Siamese cats," Hillary said, "are the most trainable breed. They are slender and elegant and they love to talk."

Harold had seven different ways of saying *meow*, according to Hillary.

That day on the playground, Dolores's classmates crowded around Hillary. They had a lot of questions. She had a lot of answers.

After school, Dolores told her older
sister, Faye, about Hillary's pedigreed cat.
"Duncan has relatives, too," Faye said.
"We just don't know who they are."

So Dolores made a pedigree for Duncan.
"Who is Her Highness Queen Isabella Fuzzkins?"
asked Faye.
"Duncan's great-grandmother, of course," said Dolores.

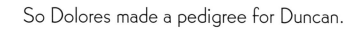

"Harold is slender and elegant,"
said Dolores later. "The trouble with
Duncan is he's too fat."
"He looks okay to me," said Faye.
"Just let Duncan be Duncan."

"He needs to eat less and talk more," said Dolores. "Harold has seven different ways of saying *meow*."

"Duncan will have a *lot* to say about his new diet," said Faye.

For the class Halloween Party, it was no surprise to anybody that Dolores and Hillary wore the same costume. They each baked special cupcakes.

But Hillary's cupcakes had red licorice whiskers on them.

In Social Studies the class was learning about ancient Egypt. Hillary raised her hand. "The ancient Egyptians worshiped their cats," she said.

A week later, for her class project Hillary unveiled a papier-mâché sarcophagus. It was a huge success.

That afternoon, Dolores told Faye about the cupcakes and the sarcophagus.

"Sounds like you two have a lot in common," said Faye.

"Hillary walks Harold every day after school," said Dolores. "How ridiculous is that!"

Then she made a leash for Duncan.

"I bet Duncan would rather take a nap," said Faye.

The next day, there was an important announcement:

ATTENTION!

Can your pet do something special?
Bring your pet to Show-and-Tell on
Pet Day. (No dangerous insects
or poisonous reptiles, please!)

The Amazing Harold

Duncan

The night before Pet Day, Dolores said, "How can Duncan compete with that big-eared wondercat, Harold?"

"Listen, Dolores," said Faye. "Just let Duncan be Duncan!"

The next morning, Dolores still hadn't thought of anything special Duncan could do for Pet Day.

After Lydia's gerbil had modeled the latest cruise wear . . .

O'er the land of the free . . .

and Jake and his rabbit had performed the national anthem . . .

and the home . . .

of the brave!

Hillary and Harold arrived. There was a buzz of excitement as she wheeled in her latest triumph of papier-mâché—a maze in the shape of King Tut's ancient Egyptian tomb.

"They say that once you enter Tut's tomb, you never come out," said Hillary. "But watch! When I blow this whistle, the amazing Harold will find his way through the maze and escape his doom in less than"—Hillary checked her stopwatch—"one minute and fifteen seconds."

START

"My, my!" said Ms. Feeny. "That's quite an ambitious project our Hillary has taken on!"
"Wow!" said almost everyone else in the class.

After Hillary gave a short tweet on her whistle, Harold began his journey.

Two minutes passed. Where was Harold?

Another minute passed. Harold's cries grew louder.
"Do you think Harold could be stuck, dear?" asked Ms. Feeny.

Then suddenly it was silent.
"I know how to get him out," said Hillary. She blew three long blasts on her whistle.

That's when Cha-cha, Chelsea's parakeet, burst into song . . .

Lilly, Luke's guinea pig, started to squeal and run in circles . . .

and Izzy, Ida's dachshund, began to bark and chase Lilly.

Soon every pet in the room was hopping or squeaking . . .

chirping or howling . . .

flying or leaping!

Except Duncan.
He had found the
perfect lap for a nap.

ZZZZZZZZZZZZZ

FINISH

Out popped Harold, right into Hillary's arms!

Everyone in class had something to say about what happened on Pet Day.

DUNCAN BREAKS
KING TUT'S
CURSE!

BY SAM

I OWE
MY LIFE TO
DUNCAN!

That is what Harold
is saying if you could
understand Siamese.
by Chelsea

MY HERO!!!!

How could I have
doubted you, Duncan?
xxx Dolores

Thank you for
saving my
Harold today.

Hillary

A few days later, Dolores announced:
"I've decided to let Duncan be Duncan."
"That's good," said Faye.
"And let Harold be Harold," said Dolores.
"Great," said Faye.

"And even let Hillary be Hillary,"
said Dolores. "Because, you
have to admit, Faye, *together*
we are truly . . .

amazing!"